THE

CLOUD

Future Chron Universe

Volume 10

From The Earth Series

Book 10

D.W. PATTERSON

Copyright © 2021 D.W. Patterson

All rights reserved

Fourteenth Printing – April, 2023

Cover - Copyright © 2023 D.W. Patterson

Cover Image – © Tom Cerny

All rights reserved. No part of this book may be reproduced in any manner whatsoever without permission, except in the case of brief quotations for the purpose of review. This is a work of fiction. Names, characters, places and events are products of the author's imagination and should not be construed as real. Any resemblance to actual events and people, living or dead, is entirely coincidental.

FOREWORD

The dates found at the beginning of most chapters do not run sequentially because of the finite speed of light and the vast spatial extent of the Star-Way. The story, though hopping from one distant location to another, is told in a logical, event-driven order. It is hoped that the non-sequential dating does not cause confusion for the reader.

Note that if a chapter does not have a date heading that chapter's action occurs at the same time as the previous chapter.

Also note that the dates are given as SE which stands for Space Era. This dating systems equates to the usual system (either AD or CE) in this story as 358 SE is the same as 2328 AD (or CE). So 358.1 SE is the first month of the year 358 or January, 2328 AD (or CE). 358.12 SE would be the twelfth month of the year 358 or December, 2328 AD (or CE).

1

358.1 SE

A powerful laser beam generated near the sun was focused on a relay station's lens seventy AU distant in the Kuiper Belt. At that relay station, the beam was again focused and sent a further seventy AU to the next relay station which refocused the beam and sent it to the next relay station, this was repeated almost fourteen-hundred times now.

Caught in that beam huge gossamer-like light-sails along with their payloads would one day be driven to accelerations of one Earth gravity. Eventually, each successive relay station would refocus the beam until other powerful lasers in the Centauri system would decelerate the sail ships the same way. Time of transit would be some two-thousand two-hundred days (five-point eight years, Earth time).

It was the biggest construction job ever undertaken by the Solar Federation, a loose alliance of the outer planets of the Solar System. A corporation set up by the Federation and based on Earth was directly responsible for building it. The construction of the Star-Way had been underway now for almost a century. And in that time the project had brought life to the outer edges of the Oort Cloud.

Excess heat from the minuscule amount of light absorbed by the relay station lenses had to be disposed of some way. Most of this heat was shunted away to a power plant built close by. Although the absorbed heat was only about one part in a million, the resulting power generated was large because of the huge power output of the lasers, the power output was in the gigawatt range. The resultant electricity was enough for a city habitat of up to two-hundred fifty-thousand people and their industrial support base.

But not all relay stations were accompanied by human settlements, most were autonomously run by Ems.

Ems, emulated human brains running on a computer, were an early form of Artificial Intelligence. The human brain imprinted as an Em could be copied any number of times, a process that was called budding. Budded Ems and the original imprint made up a family. Families sought jobs to pay for the hardware and power they needed. And to bud more Ems.

So far only one out of every five nodes was accompanied by settlements built by the Corporation. A distance of thirty-two billion miles, about the distance between Jupiter and the Sun, between settlements, meant that they were truly isolated. Even a third-generation fusion ship took over twenty days to travel from one settlement to another. And while still small the total population of the Star-Way amounted to almost four-hundred thousand people.

Besides the officially sanctioned settlements, around some of the other nodes independent settlers had gathered in small space habitats. Founded by religious, political, trans-humanist or otherwise marginalized groups they braved one of the remotest corners of space for freedom. These groups ranged in size from a few hundred to a few thousand. The Star-Way Corporation didn't approve of such settlements but didn't have the resources to patrol every node and evict illegal squatters. The Ems of those nodes were allowed to cooperate with the squatters as long as they caused no operational problems.

Mia Jackson was several kilometers from Beam Relay Station (BRS) Fourteen-Hundred. The big lenses were almost like mirrors at certain angles, six hundred meters across, thin and wispy, they glinted in what light there was this far out. At ninety-eight-thousand AU (over nine trillion miles) from the Sun, there was only starlight and the artificial lights of the work complex. These are what Mia saw reflecting off the lenses occasionally, almost as if they were waving in the breeze, but of course, there was no breeze.

Mia was waiting for first light, when the laser light from the last relay station would be refocused to this relay station. Then tests of the focusing capability of this station would be conducted. If everything turned out optimal the crew would start packing for the next build seventy AU further out.

One-third of the way to the Centauri system, thought Mia. *At the pace we're going and maybe with a little speed up, it could be less than a hundred years. I might be around to see it.*

Right now there were only two beams on their way to BRS fourteen-hundred. Beams were always used in pairs and on opposing lenses to prevent a turning force on the framework that held the lens. Eventually, for redundancy three beams each way would be used for a total of six. The beam from the Sun had been refocused by multiple lenses into multiple beams until the thirteen-hundred and ninety-eight relay station, just over nineteen hours ago, had refocused the beams toward the thirteen-hundred ninety-ninth relay station which would refocus the beams again and send them on to number fourteen-hundred where they would arrive in nine and a half hours.

Which was now, the beams of light hit the lenses. The powerful beam which had been generated from a stationary platform near old Sol was a deep violet, as the wavelength of the beam was close to the ultraviolet. Beyond the relay station, Mia could see small particles dancing in the beams. Some were being accelerated out of the beam's path while others were disappearing as they were vaporized by a portion of the thousand-trillion watts generated by the lasers. This was another advantage of the Star-Way, the sweeping and vaporizing of particles clearing a path for the light sails.

The refocused beams looked good and Mia smiled as she had over a hundred times before at each startup.

Then one of the beams "blinked".

2

Chris Martin had followed his family out into the relative emptiness of the Star-Way. The Martins, the Romeros, the Vegas and sixty other families had banded together to make the journey from Star-Way Corporation's Rutland settlement to the last unsettled node. Combining resources, they had contracted a heavy-lift fusion ship, essentially a space tug, to move their space hab and old second-generation fusion ship. After three and a half years they were nearly at the end of their journey, BRS fourteen-hundred. They would be in on the ground floor of the development that would follow the establishment of the relay station.

Chris had been twenty-six when they began, he was now over twenty-nine. He was responsible for the computer systems on-board the habitat and the fusion ship, making sure nothing happened to the hardware hosting the family of Ems that kept the rotating habitat in trim and drove the fusion ship when it was in use. It was an important responsibility and Chris took it seriously.

The Martin's habitat, which they and the other settlers named *New Start*, was a wheel-cylinder-wheel arrangement. The wheels at each end were fourteen-hundred feet in diameter and seventy feet wide. The resulting floor area was over two-million square feet. Spinning at just under two revolutions a minute provided a centrifugal force and resulting artificial gravity of nine-tenths that of Earth. Protection from radiation was provided by several feet of a moist gel substance engineered by the Ems and placed along the walls of the outer hull.

The central cylinder between the two wheels was two-hundred-fifty feet in diameter and two-hundred feet in length. It didn't have the same astounding view that the large open ones at Corporation settlements had but it did have an internal scaffolding that held plants and grew them using aeroponics, a method of growing plants that exposed their roots to the air and misted them in water and nutrients. This form of gardening was one-hundred thirty times more efficient than open sky farming back on Earth.

The cylinder provided six million square feet, half for growing, half for storage. It also spun at two revolutions per second but because of the smaller diameter only provided an artificial gravity equivalent to that of Earth's moon. The cylinder's outer walls were lined with the same gel-like material as the wheels to provide radiation protection.

The wheels themselves were honeycombed with rooms. Private apartments, workrooms, storage areas and larger workout and assembly areas. Only in the middle at the rotational axis could one move between wheels and the cylinder. The habitat was very utilitarian, practical and relatively cheap. Still, it had been three and a half years in a spinning tin can as Chris' sister Ana Sofia often said.

Chris wondered if she truly realized that they might be spending the rest of their lives in that “spinning tin can”.

"Chris," said his dad, Frank Martin. "The Captain of the tug has informed me that he is ready to begin maneuvering to decelerate. He will be decoupling the docking harness and bringing the tug around to the opposite end to slow the assembly. You need to get on board the fusion ship, undock and bring it around to re-dock where the tug is vacating."

"Okay dad, I'm on my way."

Chris didn't even take a co-pilot with him to the ship, *Last Chance,* since it was a simple matter to undock, run down the length of the cylinder and re-dock. He should be finished and back inside the *New Start* before the slow, ponderous tug was even in position at the other end.

Chris drifted down the center access way to the docking area which didn't rotate with the rest of the habitat. Boarding the ship Chris called on the ship's Em, Chance.

"Chance," said Chris. "Power up. Prepare to undock. I will take control of the ship and move it to the other end of the habitat."

"Yes Chris."

The spaceship was in motion before Chris sat down in the Captain's seat. Although the Em was perfectly capable of the maneuver, Chris took the controls and continued backing the ship away from the docking mechanism. Vectoring to the left and lifting the nose Chris soon had the ship drifting down the top side of the cylindrical habitat which he inspected as he went.

Looking to his right Chris saw the space tug giving wide berth to the habitat as it maneuvered to the opposite end. As he watched, the tug lit up in a dazzling purple light that swept from stern to bow. As fast as it had appeared the light disappeared. Chris was blinded a moment.

Closing his eyes a few seconds he looked again in the tug's direction. He could see escaping gas, smoke or fluids of some kind aft. The bow of the tug was dipping as it began to pivot downwards. The engines appeared dead, the tug adrift without attitude control.

The pivot became worse, the tug looked like a head down whale adrift. Whatever was escaping from the rear section was accelerating the pivot. The spin became more complex as the material escaping was off center and created another spin axis around the spine of the ship. Fortunately, the motion was taking the tug away from the habitat.

That's when Chris saw the escape pods. He began maneuvering the *Last Chance* towards the pods.

"Chance, prepare to pick up escape pods."

"Roger."

Each pod had the universal docking collar with which all spaceships were outfitted. The pods were maneuverable and as Chris closed on the first he saw it maneuvering towards the docking mechanism of the *Last Chance*.

Chris was busy for an hour picking up survivors from the tug which had continued its spin and continued drifting away from the habitat, there was no immediate danger to the settlers.

3

352.4 SE

Samuel S. Hampton had been CEO of the Star-Way Corporation for five years now. It was not an easy corporation to manage. Spread out across ninety-eight thousand AU, that is if the latest node had been established successfully which Samuel wouldn't know for some time. Communications with the farthest end of the Star-Way now took a year and a half. And if you wanted a response, that would take another year and a half.

Samuel wondered, *How do you manage something like that?*

Then he answered himself, *you don't.*

Samuel had brought distributed management ideas to the Corporation when he was appointed CEO. Decision making became more local, almost all decisions important in running the Star-Way had devolved to the branch offices and field managers. At first, corporate was unwilling to relinquish tight control over decisions. But eventually, they had to, as it took too long to make even the simplest decisions and distribute them across the Star-Way.

For instance, how do you choose field managers? How do you interview someone a year and a half distant, by slow-motion conferencing?

To keep the project going, decisions had to be made in at most days, not years. So now branch offices did much of the staffing and most of the operating decisions were made on-site.

The branch offices were located at settlements. Each branch was responsible for two relay stations before the settlement and two after. A territory of two-hundred eighty AU patrolled by a third generation fusion ship that took over two weeks travel time, end to end.

But if communications problems were daunting, actually sending or receiving any material from the frontier settlements along the Star-Way was an even more daunting task. Communications were almost instantaneous compared to the time required to physically ship freight or people to or from the settlements with fusion ships. And it would remain that way until the other end of the Star-Way in the Centauri system was operational and the returning beams provided a way to decelerate the sail ships.

While each settlement saw to it that it was self-sufficient as far as water and foodstuffs were concerned there was still much material that was required to outfit and keep a settlement running that had to be acquired from the outside. And when the settlement needed something the time it took to get the item depended on how far away the shipper was from that settlement. In the worst case, say from Earth to the settlement being constructed at relay station fourteen-hundred, it could take over fifteen years for a shipment to be delivered by fusion ship!

This was unacceptable, so settlements became warehouses or specialized manufacturing centers. It was unusual for a settlement to have to go much further than the four nearest settlements to purchase needed supplies. Goods could be shipped across those four settlements in as little as three months.

And with four settlements behind and four settlements in front meeting almost any need was practically guaranteed. So settlements had established quite a trading economy among themselves.

To coordinate this economy the Corporation took a small transaction fee for each trade. It also provided continuing management and representation on Earth where the settlements were registered.

Samuel was pleased with all he had accomplished in the past five years. There was much to do to make the structure more efficient but he had made a good start. Without his reconsideration of the management structure he was sure the Corporation would be struggling to survive by now instead of running a surplus on the fees from the settlements.

The only problems left seem manageable.

His personal-assistant, an ANI (Artificial Narrow Intelligence) device, usually called an Annie, alarmed. There was a message from security. It seemed there was some kind of disturbance at relay station thirteen-hundred ninety-five and its settlement. The message had been sent from the previous settlement, it was over a year and a half old. More information would follow.

Great. I don't even know what is happening out at the latest relay station build and now this at thirteen-nine-five. This is the kind of thing that keeps me up at night.

4

358.1 SE

Mia was using her Annie to communicate from the company's fusion ship to her team around the relay site, inquiring as to what could have caused the beam phenomenon she had observed.

The most compelling explanation seemed to be that the beam had intercepted a comet or asteroid momentarily as it moved in and out of the beam's path. Comets and asteroids were still plentiful even this far out in the Oort Cloud. But no one could say for sure.

Even with the best technology available it was impossible to detect, across seventy AU, all the debris that might lie in that direction. Most objects were just too small to be noticed. So it was more speculation than fact that Mia received as she queried her team as to what had caused the "blink".

Though the conjecture was reasonable, Mia wasn't satisfied. The only way to find out for sure was to go and see for herself. Mia called the Commander of the fusion ship and asked him to plot a course to investigate the region of space lying between them and the last relay station.

It would take the ship at least four days to reach the previous relay station and four days to return if they had to go that far. In the meantime, Mia informed her second in command to proceed with the beam tests while she was away.

The ship's telescopes were put into service and monitored by the on-board Ems. The Ems were much more capable than the personal-assistant Annies. They had once been at the top of the intelligence hierarchy on Earth but had lost that position when Artificial General Intelligence's (called Aggies) was developed. Most Ems migrated whenever Aggies arrived in their vicinity. Fortunately for Ems, Aggies, because of their hardware requirements and interests, had yet to make it much past the orbit of Jupiter.

Mia instructed the Ems to watch for any body the size of a small asteroid or any debris indicating the breakup of such a body. She would use her Annie to monitor the findings from her quarters.

Third generation fusion ships, which owed their development to the Aggies of Earth, were a great improvement over the old second-generation ships. They were nearly a hundred times faster, they were larger and roomier, and they had a larger habitat wheel which provided artificial gravity without the dizzying effect that the smaller wheels of the older generation sometimes caused.

Their cabins were roomier and more comfortable too, especially if you were the head of Star-Way Corporation's construction department as was Mia. She soon fell asleep in her comfortable bed.

Mia's Annie alarmed. She awoke slowly, it seemed she had just gone to sleep. She looked at her Annie. It was just after oh-two-hundred hours. Mia couldn't have been asleep for more than an hour.

She sat up in bed. The telescope monitors were reporting a small elongated asteroid at the extreme distance of detection, seventeen AU. Time of rendezvous would be approximately twelve hours.

Wait, that can't be right unless, thought Mia.

She queried her Annie. "That is correct," said the Annie. "Intercept will be in approximately twelve-point two-four hours."

"How can that be," said Mia. "We aren't traveling fast enough unless the object is approaching us ...."

"The object is approaching us at one-tenth of light-speed," said her Annie. "On a heading that is directly towards this ship."

Mia put down her Annie.

What in the world?

After rescuing the men in the escape pods Chris had docked the *Last Chance* at the same docking port as before. The men had already transferred to the habitat when Chris instructed the ship's Em to keep the fusion rocket firing. Chris knew it wasn't enough to stop the heavy habitat before it passed relay station fourteen-hundred but it was all he could do for now.

Chris's dad met him as he entered the cafeteria area.

"You okay son?"

"I'm fine dad, a little tired and hungry. How are the men from the tug?"

"You did good son, you did all you could, we'll just have to ride this out. As far as the tug crew, except for the Captain and the control center personnel, they are all fine. It seems that no one made it out of the control center."

Mia was in the control center of the company ship. Hours had passed since the first sighting of the object. One of the crew called her and the Captain over to his console. Captain Bering was an auggie, augmented human. It was uncommon to meet very many auggies as most people living in the physical world carried no or very few augmentations. Most augmented reality enthusiasts were more likely to not stop with augmentations for their bodies but end up in the meta-verse, the virtual reality world managed by the Aggies on Earth.

Captain Bering had augmented for job efficiency. Implants directly linked his auditory system with the ship's Em. Through this link, the Captain and Em could communicate three to four times faster than most people could speak. The only downside to the link was that the Captain would sometimes seem to be distracted.

The crew member that had called them cast his screen to holo mode. He pointed to the object they were trying to intercept. In one motion his hand spread wide and the holo expanded. Then he pointed to the object.

"Can you tell what it is?" asked Mia.

"Not yet ma'am," replied the crew member.

The ship's Em had identified the object and passed that information along through the Captain's auditory channel. It was a space habitat, a habitat large enough for dozens if not hundreds of people, a habitat that shouldn't be this far out.

"Squatters," said the Captain.

"What do you mean?" said Mia.

"That's a space habitat probably with dozens of people aboard. Why else would it be this far out?"

"Sir," said the navigator. "I have plotted the course of the object. It is headed directly towards relay station fourteen-hundred."

"What do you mean," said Mia. "Is the station in danger?"

"Ma'am, I can't tell. All I know is that its course will take it very close to the complex, uncomfortably close."

5

Mia and the Captain discussed the situation in the remaining time before intercept.

"Captain we absolutely must deflect that habitat's course."

"Ms. Jackson," began Captain Bering. He paused momentarily looking lost.

"We have six-point two hours to act. By the time we can dock and have any influence on that tin can's course it will be an hour less. I am willing to try. But I'm doubtful we can deflect or slow the habitat enough to completely eliminate the danger to the station."

The warnings went off in the control room of the *Last Chance*. An object was approaching on an intercept course at a speed of point one light-speed at four AU. Chris and his dad along with Tomas Romero and a couple of others were there.

"Chris," said his dad. "Do you think you can get anything with the telescopes? Let us see what is approaching?"

"I don't know dad, I'll try."

Chris remotely focused the most powerful telescope aboard the *Last Chance* on the approaching object. He fed the telescope's output into his Annie and requested an analysis. The Annie found it impossible to analyze yet, the image was too small, only a pixel or two. But that gave him enough information to speculate.

He looked up from his Annie.

"There isn't enough resolution to specify yet dad. But I can tell you that at this distance if the telescope can only resolve a pixel or two we are probably dealing with a fusion ship. Nothing else that size would be out this far. And if it were bigger we would have been able to resolve it."

"Makes sense son. Well, we won't have to worry about a collision then, a fusion ship should be able to easily maneuver around us."

At a distance of about four times that of the Earth from its moon, the corporate fusion ship tried to communicate with the *Last Chance.*

"Habitat," said Captain Bering into the camera. "This is Star-Way Corporation's ship *Far Path*, over."

Frank Martin spoke for the *Last Chance* five seconds later. "*Far Path* this is the *Last Chance* habitat. We note that you are on an intercept course. What can we do for you?"

After a delay, the Captain said, "We are aware of our course *Last Chance*. We are also aware that your course will take you dangerously close to the Corporation's relay station fourteen-hundred. We believe it is imperative that you alter your course to lessen the danger to the relay station."

"Captain this is Frank Martin Council Head of the *Last Chance*. We have suffered an accident. The tug that was piloting us was destroyed by what appeared to be a purple ray. And we haven't the thrust to vector away from our current course."

The Captain turned aside to Mia.

"The cause of the 'blink,'" he whispered. She nodded.

Turning back to the camera he said, "Understood *Last Chance*. We will soon be there and will assist in deflecting the habitat away from the relay station."

Chris and his dad glanced at each other. Frank Martin said, "Captain we understand your concern. But you can't just vector us into empty space. We are on course towards relay station fourteen-hundred because the relay station is our original destination."

"Squatters," said Mia into the camera.

"Ma'am," said Chris before his dad could speak. "We have no intention of 'squatting'. We intend to be the first citizens of *Ciudad del Camino Dorado* when the corporation establishes it."

"City of the Golden Way? You've already given it a name?"

"We will suggest that name, yes. We know the Corporation has naming rights."

"That's right mister and the Corporation also has the right to decide who is and who isn't a citizen of one of its settlements."

"We understand that ma'am. But getting back to your plan to deflect us. As my dad said, you can't just vector us into empty space. We wouldn't survive."

Mia looked at the Captain and signaled for him to follow her.

The Captain turned to the camera and said, "We'll get back to you *Last Chance*."

"Captain we have a problem. They are right, we can't just vector them off into space. We are inadvertently responsible for them being in the situation they are in. I don't know how the beam disrupted their tug but I have no reason to doubt them. However, we can't let that tin can damage the relay station either. Do you have any ideas?"

"Ms. Jackson," said the Captain who then paused. "I noticed they have an old second-generation fusion ship. We could use that to change the direction vector of the habitat slightly by having it dock at the back end and use its attitude rockets to alter the habitat's course while we are at the other end pushing with full thrust to cancel its forward momentum. We should miss the relay station site by six-point seven kilometers."

"That sounds like a great plan Captain."

"But we will not be able to halt the habitat's progress until we are well beyond the relay station. We will then have to push them back to the area of the relay station. All of this effort will cost us a loss of four point two days and the loss of enough fuel that we will need to return to a settlement to refuel."

"How long Captain?"

"Your building plans will be delayed one and a half months maybe more."

"Maybe?"

"Yes, there are too many variables involved to be more precise."

Mia just shook her head.

6

350.10 SE

Doc Garcia hadn't planned for it to turn out this way but once the movement was started it took on a life of its own. People rallied to the cause as if they had only been waiting for the chance. Even though the settlement hadn't been established for long, most of the people making up the citizenry had been under Corporate supervision at previous settlements. And all had developed a distaste for the Corporation's governance.

Freedom had attracted them, freedom had lured them nine trillion miles into a void dangerously unforgiving to human life. And once they arrived they found the same regulations and levies on their lives and fortunes that they thought they had left behind. The Corporation exacted its fees, it made claims on their time and energy just as any government would. To anyone that knew the body politic of the settlement of thirteen-nine-five the rush to freedom when self-determination was placed within their reach would have been no surprise.

But Doc Garcia had been surprised and those in his circle of influence had been surprised. They had sought to reduce the worse of the restrictive regulations that the Corporation imposed, they had sought to increase their power and wealth as the local management, but a declaration of autonomy was not what they had sought. It was what they had been forced to accept to stay ahead of the clambering masses and maintain their positions as the leaders of those masses, leaders that were worried and fearful.

"I know it is something that Corporate will have to act upon Doc. But what will happen when they do? That's what I'm worried about," said Enrique Lopez, acting Comptroller of the settlement.

"Not much Enrique. We're too far away from Earth and I doubt that the nearest Corporate settlements will be interested in using force to bring us in line, so to speak."

"But how about economic retaliation?"

"Possible, but we have very important leverage against such action."

"The relay station?"

"Exactly, they need to keep the relay station functioning and as long as we agree to support their efforts, or at least not to interfere with their efforts, I don't think they will do anything to create an adversarial atmosphere."

Doc Garcia drew up the contract to send to the Board of Directors for the Star-Way Corporation. He stated at the beginning of the document that from this day forward the settlement at relay station thirteen-nine-five, henceforth to be known as *Ciudad de las Estrellas*, City of the Stars, would be an independent administrative territory. The city was willing to be an associate of the Star-Way Corporation with special consideration given. But the current financial structure was unsustainable.

The city government proposed that a reasonable tax on the relay station should be paid by the Corporation. However, this tax would be waved for twenty years in return for the city's appropriation of the settlement's power station and other assets.

There were many more details in the contract that Doc wouldn't cover in this message to the board, those were for the lawyers to hammer out. He closed the message by reiterating that the City of the Stars hoped for a very close working relationship with the Star-Way Corporation and that the city also hoped for a quick contract approval.

A year and a half, thought Garcia. By the time the Board of Directors received his contract proposal the city will be *de facto* independent. There really wasn't a choice for the Star-Way Corporation. They would either approve the contract that Doc sent them or risk the loss of an important node in their system. A loss that would cripple the entire enterprise.

7

358.3 SE

The *Far Path* had pushed the habitat back to relay station fourteen-hundred. As the relay station came into view Mia immediately noticed the lack of beam.

"Where's the beam?" she said to Captain Bering.

"I don't know," he responded.

"Captain, get me Jim on the comm immediately. I'll take the call in my quarters."

Mia's Annie announced the incoming call.

"Mia, this is Jim."

Jim was Mia's second in command.

"Jim where is the beam?"

"We think something happened at thirteen-nine-five while you were looking for that habitat you brought back. They either can't or won't answer our calls. All other intermediate relays have responded."

"So they've cut off my beam, have they. Well we'll need to do something about that won't we?"

"Right boss."

Mia had invited Captain Bering along with her senior staff to a conference aboard the *Far Path*.

"Gentlemen," she began. "We have a choice to make. We can either wait for instruction from the Corporation which could come at any time or three years from now when we get back an answer to the message I just sent the Board. Or we can come up with a plan ourselves."

"Mia," said the Captain. "I take it when you say we can come up with a plan, you mean a plan to get the beam back online?"

"Of course Captain."

"And that means getting thirteen-nine-five to restore operation of their relay station. If they deliberately cut the beam, I for one don't think they will restore it just because we ask nicely."

"I realize that Captain. If that is the case, I won't be asking nicely but emphatically."

"They might say no. What then?"

"Then we will take the relay station and operate it ourselves."

"By force?" said a beam engineer.

"If necessary," said Mia.

"We have no weapons for such an assignment."

"We have all the weapons we need," said Mia. "Before me is a room full of the finest engineering minds anywhere. If we can't come up with a plan to get the beam back online, then I doubt anyone can."

8

352.6 SE

Samuel S. Hampton was trying his best to get control of the board meeting. Directors and majority investors were shouting at each other. Samuel picked up the large company ledger and slammed it on the conference table.

"Quiet," he said. "Quiet gentlemen, please!"

"Samuel," said George Samson of Samson Equity. "You know how much my company has invested in this project. This is a loss we simply can't afford. We still have very little income coming back. What are you going to do about it?"

"George I am going to make sure that node stays online. That's what I am going to do about it."

"How? It's what? A year and a half communications time to node thirteen-nine-five? And if I'm not mistaken over fifteen years by fusion ship."

"Fifteen years!" said another. "We'll be out of business and broke."

"Hold on, hold on," said Samuel. "I've been discussing the problem with our chief engineer. He has an idea."

Samuel took out his Annie. "Miriam, would you send Horace in."

"Yes sir."

Horace Mann, Chief Engineer for Star-Way Corporation came into the room. He was dressed in his usual dark slacks, white shirt and loose tie.

"Gentlemen, for those of you who haven't met him, this is our Head of Engineering, Horace Mann. Horace would you explain your idea about how to use the Star-Way to resolve our problem in a timely manner."

"Yes Samuel, and thank you."

"Gentlemen, as you know, we had originally planned to implement sail traffic when we had established laser beams in the Centauri system. However, there is a way that we can start up the Star-Way now."

"How?" said Samson.

"Sir, as you know the focus lenses used at each node act to re-focus and relay the beam further. However under typical operation, those lenses will also bend the beam to one side, this is how they will power the light sails when the time comes. As a matter of fact they can bend the beam one-hundred and eighty degrees if necessary. In other words reflect the beam back the way it came."

"And exactly how does that solve our problem?" asked one of the Directors impatiently.

"It will be apparent shortly. I am going into some detail because I want you gentlemen to understand why we will need another round of investments."

"What!" said Samson. "More money! Samuel is he crazy?"

"Hold on George, hear the boy out. His idea is the only one we have that will save what we already have invested."

"Thank you Mr. Hampton. As I was saying gentlemen. We can reflect a beam back with the lens, one-hundred eighty degrees, back to the previous relay station's lens that would normally focus a beam from the Centauri lasers.

"So we now have one beam going in one direction and if it is reflected back the other way when it reaches the end of the Star-Way which in this case will be BRS thirteen-nine-four we will have a two-way transportation system."

"Excellent," said a Director. "So now we can accelerate and decelerate a light sail along the Star-Way. Right?"

"You are right, but there is a problem. There is no way to prevent the torque from the impinging beams from destabilizing the relay stations eventually. That and redundancy, are the reasons we have three pairs of beams in our design. It can be shown that by pairing the beams in a hexagonal geometry the resultant torque will be at a minimum. Reducing the station keeping needs of each relay station."

"Okay," said Samson. "I understand now why you want more money. We need to finish up and bring the last two lasers on line. Is that what you mean by further investment?"

"Yes sir."

"How long?" said Samson.

“I believe we can have the additional lasers ready within a month. At the same time we can get the prototype sail ready. Its cargo will be one of the Corporation's fusion ships modified for such a long voyage. The security force will also be readied. After a month of preparation we will start the journey.”

“What about the other side? How will they know to reverse the beams.”

“We will send a message immediately to the relay stations. At the longest it will take about a year and a half for the message to reach the farthest operational relay station along with the new beams. By that time half of the relay stations will be prepared to reflect the beams back.

“Now the sail will take almost three years to make it to thirteen-nine-four at an acceleration and deceleration of one Earth gravity. So the sail will be halfway to the end of its journey when the message reaches thirteen-nine-four. But every relay station will be prepared to turn-around the beams at the proper time if needed until the sail comes to a full stop at thirteen-nine-four.

“Then the fusion ship will continue on its way to thirteen-nine-five under its own power and hopefully bring that relay station back online.”

“Thank you Horace,” said Samuel. “I'm sure there are many more technical details that you could mention but I think you have described the situation in enough detail for us to take a vote.”

Mann left the room.

"Okay," said Samuel. "Let's vote."

The vote was nineteen to one in favor of Mann's plan.

9

"Okay let me get this straight," said Larry Owens. "They're gonna blast us off into space before they have a way of stopping the ship."

"Essentially you are right sir," said Wayne Blackwell.

"I don't know who is crazier. The guys running this place or me for working here."

"Well there is a plan," said Wayne. "We accelerate at one Earth gravity for approximately a year and a half. Then we turn the sail around and decelerate for a year and a half and we are there. However, because it takes a year and a half for a radio message to get to what is currently the other end of the Star-Way some of the intermediate relay stations will have to apply the decelerating beam until the final station comes online.

"The interesting thing is that the intermediate stations will have to reflect the beam to decelerate us and once we are past them they will have to transmit that beam further on. At about three-quarters of the way this beam manipulation can cease as the beam from the last relay station, I think thirteen-nine-four, will have reached our position at the time. From there on the Star-Way will act pretty much as it was designed."

"I still don't understand," said Larry. "It sounds like a lot of careful timing and if even a few stations fail to decelerate us we go flying off towards the Centauri System."

"Oh well, in that case we'll have plenty of time to worry. And don't forget we'll be the first to see the Centauri System."

"Yeah, if the food and water last."

"As far as I know the aeroponic gardens can be kept going indefinitely, and water will be available as long as we keep the recycling systems working,"

"More work," moaned Larry.

"With a good purpose, I think you will agree."

"I suppose, and even if the trip goes as planned I suppose they have a workable plan when we get to thirteen-nine-five. Right?"

"Of course. We simply board the relay station and put it back into operation. Very non-confrontational."

Larry shook his head.

The sail deployed. One kilometer across it was made of lithium-beryllium nanotubes weaved like an old straw hat. The nanotubes were coated in graphene to dissipate the heat of the beam. As big as it was the sail still weighed less than thirty-two tonnes.

As the sail-bots scurried across the material like spiders, unrolling it, the pressure of the solar light bowed the sail into its final conical shape. Once fully deployed the sail would be set rotating very slowly. Under rotation, the heavier rim elements would act to pull the sail taut and keep it in shape.

The fusion ship was tethered one-kilometer sun-ward of the sail. The ship was using its attitude control rockets to hold the sail in position as it deployed. The ship was part of the sail's active stability system providing a way to steer the whole structure, like the rudder on a boat. Also providing stability were rows and rows of pivoting nanotubes, opening and closing like flaps on a plane to vector the light pressure and keep the sail in trim.

The stability system was controlled by a dozen Ems making split-second decisions as to the pivots and ship's attitude rockets.

The relay stations ahead of the sail's position would be sweeping the beam to clear the sail lane of any debris too small to be detected. Even with this safety precaution, there was still a small possibility of collision. To deal with this the sail had a built-in ability to heal itself should something strike it. Holes up to ten centimeters across could be rewoven by the sail-bots.

The ship would accelerate in sunlight until the laser was turned on and then the beam would quickly bring the sail's acceleration up to one Earth gravity. The ship itself had a reinforced front and rear buffer and a magnetic sweep system at both ends to push charged and uncharged particles out of its way.

The ship's common rooms were in what was called the gravity ring. At a diameter of one-hundred-fifty meters, the ring could be rotated to provide an artificial gravity of three-tenths Earth normal. When under beam acceleration the rooms were rotated so that the floor was to the back of the ship. When stationary or under low acceleration the rooms were rotated so that the floor was outward. The ring could then be spun up to provide artificial gravity. At launch, the rooms were rotated to the back.

Larry was the first to notice the very small acceleration as the fusion ship stopped holding the sail back. Small items like his Annie that were already floating tended to move backward in relation to the bunk room. Larry wasn't sure if he was happy to be underway.

10

354.3 SE

Much had happened in *Ciudad de las Estrellas* in the over four years since Doc Garcia sent the Declaration of Freedom to corporate. For one thing, the City Council had been elected with Doc Garcia as its head. The first act of the City Council was to declare all Corporation property to be public property except for the relay station. The Corporation was reimbursed for its property by the corporate tax holiday as spelled out in the Declaration document.

Private residences that at one time were the Corporation's property were given to the residents for the cost of the first year's property tax. The relay station was allowed to continue to operate for now. The Em operating the relay station cooperated with the new government as the new instructions did not directly interfere with the station. The Em awaited updated instructions from corporate before it took any other actions.

Garcia and Enrique Lopez were sharing a glass of wine outside the Garcia's apartment on the terrace. The wives were inside preparing dinner.

The Garcia's apartment was in the original habitat. A cylindrical form that was fourteen-hundred feet in diameter and seven-thousand feet in length. Spinning at somewhat less than two revolutions per minute the artificial gravity felt like nine-tenths that of Earth. Over five-thousand acres of livable surface area could support up to two-hundred thousand people though the settlement had only about twenty thousand now.

The Garcia's apartment like most of the apartments was a terraced design taking advantage of the curvature of the habitat. At twelve-hundred square-feet it was quite roomy for two people. The terracing design allowed for a nice outdoor veranda. The Garcia's were older and without children, residents with children had larger apartments.

Of the over two-hundred million square feet available, aeroponic gardening used only twenty percent of the area to support a fully populated cylinder. Housing took another fifty percent leaving thirty percent of the cylinder's square footage or over sixty million square feet for commercial endeavors and public lands.

Enrique who owned one of the food markets in the commercial center was talking.

"Doc as a business owner one of the things that concerns me about this freedom declaration is that it places us outside the mainstream. It doesn't lend itself to attracting new settlers. I worry about how the settlement will continue growing."

"Enrique my friend, once we get a firm commitment from the Corporation I don't think we will be viewed as outside the bounds of normal. We just need to be patient until the contract is approved."

"Well, since you bring it up. Where do we sit with the contract?"

"I haven't seen it yet."

“Shouldn't we have seen it a couple of months ago?”

“If the Corporation had sent the contract as soon as possible that's true. But let's not forget, it is a corporation and doing anything in a hurry is against standard operating procedure. So I'm not concerned yet.”

A few months after his conversation with Enrique, Doc Garcia found himself in a contentious Council meeting.

“It is absolutely apparent to me Council Head Garcia,” said Council Member Michelle Rodriguez, “that we are not going to receive a response to our contract proposal from the Star-Way Corporation. Now, I think it is judicious and I believe imperative that we prepare for the worse response possible.”

“Yes Ms. Rodriguez,” said Garcia. “And what would that 'worse response' be?”

“I believe that the Corporation intends to take some kind of action to restore its authority here. What that action might be, I don't know, but we need to take measures to prepare for the worse.”

“I suppose the worse, as you call it but do not explicitly state it, is some kind of action, some kind of forceful action?”

“I don't think it is beyond reason.”

“Very well, Ms. Rodriguez I appoint you to lead a commission to come up with some precautions that the city can take in case the worse of your suspicions comes true.”

"Very well Council Head Garcia, I propose that we gain control of the relay station and use it as a bargaining chip. Killing the beam if necessary."

11

358.4 SE

The Captain was scanning the settlement with the long-distance sensors of the *Far Path*. Something was happening. The electromagnetic and long-distance scope indicated laser fire. The Captain through the use of his auggies was convinced that a firefight had erupted at the settlement. He called Mia to the bridge.

When she entered the bridge the Captain took her aside and told her what he thought was happening.

“I don't understand,” said Mia. “Who would be doing such a thing?”

“I'm not sure,” said Captain Bering. “I hesitate to establish a comm-link since I don't know who may be responsible. But we will be within range in a few minutes and we'll know then.”

Mia shook her head.

Who could it be, she wondered. *I hope the relay station is okay.*

It was beyond her comprehension that such a thing could be happening. It was unacceptable.

A few minutes passed and the long-range scope could finally resolve the settlement. There was definitely laser fire from a fusion ship that looked to be strafing the city habitat. As the *Far Path* got closer another smaller fusion ship became visible. It looked to be leaving a docking berth on the habitat. The smaller ship started slowly but was soon undoubtedly on an intercept course to the larger ship.

As the larger ship came around that end of the habitat cylinder the smaller ship literally seemed to jump straight at it. The smaller ship struck the larger one just behind the wheel between it and the fusion engines. The larger ship began to break up but the fusion engines kept firing. The engines caused the wreckage to begin a tight spin which eventually caused it to break apart into three pieces. The front and habitat wheel of the larger ship careened off in one direction, the fusion engine of the big ship, now quiet, spun in another direction, the smaller ship went between the other two pieces spinning out of control and grazed the City of the Stars habitat.

Mia was shocked. The Captain was monitoring the wheel section of the big ship as it began to break up. Finally, just before complete disintegration, he found what he was looking for.

"Helmsman," said the Captain. "Plot a course for the escape pod coming out of that wreckage."

It was another twenty minutes before the *Far Path* had the escape pod docked and transferred its only occupant to sickbay.

The Captain and Mia were there as the survivor came around.

Mia said, "You are aboard the Star-Way Corporation ship *Far Path*. The doctor says you will be okay. Can you tell us your name and what happened?"

The man looked from Mia to the Captain and back again.

“I resign,” he said and fell quiet.

“Yes, I understand, but won't you please tell me what happened.”

“My name is Larry Owens and I was assigned to a security detail sent by the Corporation to enforce the existing contract with this settlement. We spent nearly three years accelerating and decelerating to get here. And I can tell you it was hell. I'll never go through that again.”

“Decelerating?” said the Captain.

“That's right, the geniuses back at Corporate figured out a way to reflect the beam at node thirteen-nine-four so that it could stop us there. We continued under ship's power to this settlement.”

The Captain looked at Mia.

She said, “It's been discussed before. It's tricky but I guess they felt it was necessary.”

“And what were you suppose to do when you got here?” the Captain asked.

“Like I said, enforce the contract by any means necessary. As far as I know the board rejected the settlement's claim to independence.”

“I see,” said Mia. “But the battle, why?”

“I don't think the Captain of my ship expected to go into battle. Something happened during negotiations, the settlement threatened our ship. At that point, the Captain delivered an ultimatum. I'm not sure what happened after that, I wasn't privy to that information I'm just a grunt."

"Are there any other survivors?" he asked.

"I'm afraid not," said the Captain. "We've been scanning the area ever since the incident and no other escape pods have turned up."

"Old Blackwell," said Owens shaking his head. "He's the reason I'm here. We were down in our bunk room when we heard the charge-discharge of the laser weapon. Wayne suggested that we should move closer to an escape pod. But on the way there the ship shook violently, we were thrown off our feet. Wayne hit his head when he went down. He was dead before I got to him.

"I boarded the escape pod and was just about to release it when the ship went into a violent spin. I was knocked unconscious. I guess I must have pulled the handle as I passed out. Poor Wayne, he saved my life."

The doctor motioned for Mia and the Captain to leave.

Mia said, "Thank you Larry. You get some rest and let the doctor do his magic. Just one more thing, how many others were aboard your ship?"

"There were fifty in the security detail plus the ship's crew, however many that might be, I don't know for sure."

"Okay, rest now, we'll see you later."

Outside sickbay, Mia said to the Captain, "We've got to stop this here and now. Too many lives have already been lost. This is not the way to achieve Corporate goals."

"It sounds like the Corporation wants to enforce the existing contract and not renegotiate. I don't have the authority to countermand," said the Captain.

"No, but I do," said Mia.

12

358.5 SE

"I understand what you are saying Ms. Jackson," said Council Head Garcia. "But for us the real question is that should we accept the terms of the contract you offer will the Board of Directors of the Corporation feel bound to accept?"

"I assure you Council Head Garcia that should you approve the contract that I have proposed, that the council has modified for damages, and that I then approved, the Corporation will accept it. You see it is in the bylaws of the Star-Way Corporation that should a field operative with board credentials, such as I, feel it necessary to modify a contract to further the Corporation's interests then said contract is binding upon the Corporation. The Corporation's only recourse is to fire me. It must live up to the contract through the contract's lifetime."

"Very well Ms. Jackson. The Council will take your word. If you would give us just a little time to discuss this among ourselves we will try to have you an answer no later than midnight, settlement time."

"Thank you."

Outside the council chambers, Mia and the Captain passed only a few robots rolling along as they walked the tree-lined path. The trees on the City of the Stars were not as large as on some of the other habitats that Mia had seen. These were no more than twenty feet tall. It was in keeping with the smaller size of this cylinder. At fourteen-hundred feet in diameter and somewhat over a mile in length it just didn't have the scope of the larger cylinders, the largest being four miles across and twenty miles in length where some three million people could live.

The cylinder was also not as bright since almost all lighting was artificial and had to be carefully rationed. Looking up at the lights on the far side of the cylinder caused Mia to feel a moment of vertigo because they seemed so close and vivid. It was nothing like the large cylinders where the other side was washed out or blocked by cloudiness.

"You okay?" asked the Captain.

"I'm fine," said Mia. "Just a bit of vertigo when I looked up."

"I know what you mean. I feel it too. I mean this is a nice settlement but the size makes me feel uncomfortable. I'm more at home aboard the *Far Path* than here."

"These people have made a sacrifice to push civilization this far from Earth. They deserve a break."

The council had agreed to the new contract. They got the freedom they wanted, the assignment of the settlement to the settlers. The Corporation maintained control of the relay station and was responsible for its operation. The original agreement offered by the settlers was amended so that instead of twenty years of tax deferral the Corporation only got fifteen years because of the damage the attack had caused. The Corporation also took complete responsibility for the loss of lives on both sides that had ensued.

The *Far Path* was on its way back to relay station fourteen-hundred. Mia had left most of her men at relay station thirteen-nine-five to get it back in operation with the help of its Ems. Once they were in communication range she placed a call to the Martin's habitat at fourteen-hundred.

"Is that you Mr. Martin," said Mia.

"This is Chris Martin Ms. Jackson, dad is not available right now."

"Oh good, Chris then. As you probably know the contract has been made with node thirteen-nine-five. But you probably don't know how that could affect you, your family and the rest of the families aboard the *Last Chance*."

"How's that Ms. Jackson?"

"Well according to the contract the Corporation is responsible for providing the operations personnel for the relay station at thirteen-nine-five. Though we could leave it to the Ems and their robots, as you know we like to keep humans in the loop whenever possible. So, I was hoping that those aboard the *Last Chance* would be willing to take the job.

"The settlement has agreed to take all of you and provide room and board which the Corporation will pay for. And those working at the relay station will, of course, be on the corporate payroll. Others will find jobs at the settlement.

"Do you think those aboard can give me an answer by tomorrow?"

“I'll take it up immediately with my dad, he can bring it to the Council and we should be able to have a habitat wide meeting and give you an answer within that time frame.”

“Very good Chris, I will see you and the others tomorrow.”

13

360.1 SE

Samuel Hampton was packing up his office. He had officially resigned that morning. He had been CEO of Star-Way Corporation for twelve years, it had been seven years since the board had made the decision to enforce the corporate contract with thirteen-nine-five. He had agreed with the decision at the time but had regretted the subsequent turn of events.

He still marveled that the Corporation could keep going.

Just think, seven years ago we made a fateful decision and only now are we being held accountable. How can you run such a corporation?

He thought he had solved the problem twelve years ago but he had been wrong.

He and the other members of the Board and the Corporation itself would be tied up by civil cases for many years. The families of the men that had died on that ill-fated ship and the families of those that had died on the habitat were suing.

Strange, it seems like another lifetime now.

He looked around the office one last time. Then he closed the door.

He wondered if the new CEO would fair any better or if the Star-Way Corporation would even survive.

Chris Martin had taken the job with Star-Way Corporation to monitor the operation of the relay station. He and a dozen others from the *Last Chance* had been hired to man the station around the clock.

There really wasn't much to do. The Em and its robots took care of most of the chores. Chris and the others' duties consisted of reviewing the Em's decisions and the robot's work. Sometimes there was some software to herd through the software Em.

Chris's sister Ana Sofia had gotten married a few months before and Chris was dating a woman from the settlement. All in all the settlers aboard the *Last Chance* had found just what they were looking for.

Mia hadn't yet heard from the Corporation about the contract and the incident at thirteen-nine-five. Until she heard she had decided to continue as before. Building relay stations was her life.

The construction of relay stations had been delayed a few months after the terrible incident at thirteen-nine-five but with much effort, Mia had gotten it going again. In the year since the builds had restarted her and her team had finished another six.

She was in the Corporation's fusion ship awaiting first light at fourteen-zero-six. She was thinking back to the many first lights she had seen and wondered how many more awaited her. Then there it was, the always beautiful deep purple beams from trillions of miles away. The lenses of the relay station focused the beams further on where dust particles reflected them, creating a kind of purple rain.

The beams looked good, the focus looked good, Mia was pleased.

AFTERWORD

The completion of the Star-Way is taken up in the next Future Chron story, the short novel *First Interstellar.*

The Ems first appeared in the story *Vigilance* and were developed further in *To Tend and Watch Over.* They along with the more powerful Artificial General Intelligence that I call Aggie, were important in the story *Freedom From Want.*

The idea of the Ems was suggested to me by the book *The Age of Em* by Robin Hanson.

The idea of the Star-Way was taken from a paper by Charles Quarra called *A Light Bridge to Nearby Stars.*

ABOUT THE AUTHOR

D.W. Patterson lives in the USA with his beautiful wife Sarah. He studied physics and read classic science fiction in college and then worked for many years as an electronic design engineer.

Now he's trying to write stories like the ones he once loved. See his website: dwpatterson.com for more information.

Hard Science Fiction – Old School.

Human – Generated Content.

Also By This Author:

The Future Chron Universe:

To date the Future Chron Universe has:

51 Amazon Top 100's

(15 in the Top 10)

In chronological order.

Volume numbers indicate Universe order.

Book numbers indicate Series order.

From The Earth Series

(Novellas except where noted):

Volume 1, Book 1 – ***Whatsoever You Do***

Volume 2, Book 2 – ***War Through The Pines***

Volume 3, Book 3 – ***Vigilance***

Volume 4, Book 4 – ***To Tend And Watch Over***

Volume 5, Book 5 – ***Union***

Volume 6, Book 6 – ***Circle Of Retribution***

Volume 7, Book 7 – ***Freedom From Want***

Volume 8, Book 8 – *Break Up*

Volume 9, Book 9 – *Kuiper Station*

Volume 10, Book 10 – *The Cloud*

Volume 11, Book 11 – *First Interstellar* – A Short Novel

Wormhole Series

(Novels):

Volume 12, Book 1 – *Mach's Metric*

Volume 13, Book 2 – *Mach's Mission*

Open Space Series

(Short Stories):

Volume 14, Book 1 – *Open Space*

Volume 15, Book 2 – *The Old World*

Volume 16, Book 3 – *Insurrect*

Volume 17, Book 4 – *Second Beam*

Volume 18, Book 5 – *All For One*

Volume 19, Book 6 – *One For All*

Volume 20, Book 7 – *Shotgun*

Volume 21, Book 8 – *Allison*

To The Stars Series

(Novellas):

Volume 22, Book 1 – *First One Hundred*

Volume 23, Book 2 – *First Dark Ages*

Volume 24, Book 3 – *Second One Hundred*

Volume 25, Book 4 – *Second Dark Ages*

Volume 26, Book 5 – *Path Of The Long March*

Wormhole Series

(Novel):

Volume 27, Book 3 – *Mach's Legacy*

Robot Series

(Novels):

Volume 28, Book 1 – *Spin-Two*

Volume 29, Book 2 – *Robot Planet*

Volume 30, Book 3 – *The Lattice Of Space*

Time Series

(Novels):

Volume 31, Book 1 – *Time Wars*

Volume 32, Book 2 – *Time's End*

Volume 33, Book 3 – *Frozen Time*

The Remembered Earth Universe:

To date the Remembered Earth Universe has:

8 Amazon Top 100's

Cislunar Series

(Short Stories):

Volume 1, Book 1 – *US Tugs*

Volume 2, Book 2 – *Prototype*

Volume 3, Book 3 – *L1 Or Bust*

Volume 4, Book 4 – *Guidance Box*

Volume 5, Book 5 – *Air Brakes*

Volume 6, Book 6 – *View Point*

Volume 7, Book 7 – *Space Truck*

Volume 8, Book 8 – *Dark Side* – *In Progress*

The Manifold Earth Universe:

Volume 1, Book 1 – *The Realm* – *In Progress*

Don't miss out!

Visit the website below and you can sign up to receive emails whenever D.W. Patterson publishes a new book. There's no charge and no obligation.

https://books2read.com/r/B-A-DPWE-SYFJC

BOOKS 2 READ

Connecting independent readers to independent writers.

www.ingramcontent.com/pod-product-compliance
Lightning Source LLC
LaVergne TN
LVHW010120170826
845678LV00012B/2516

* 9 7 9 8 2 2 3 1 3 9 9 7 3 *